TOO NOISY!

malachy doyle
ed vere

WALKER BOOKS
AND SUBSIDIARIES
LONDON · BOSTON · SYDNEY · AUCKLAND

FIRST PUBLISHED 2012 BY WALKER BOOKS LTD, 87 VAUXHALL WALK, LONDON SE11 5HJ · 2 4 6 8 10 9 7 5 3 1 · THIS EDITION PUBLISHED 2013 · TEXT © 2012 MALACHY DOYLE · ILLUSTRATIONS © 2012 ED VERE · THE RIGHT OF MALACHY DOYLE AND ED VERE TO BE IDENTIFIED AS AUTHOR AND ILLUSTRATOR RESPECTIVELY OF THIS WORK HAS BEEN ASSERTED BY THEM IN ACCORDANCE WITH THE COPYRIGHT, DESIGNS AND PATENTS ACT 1988 · THIS BOOK HAS BEEN TYPESET IN NEUTRAFACE MEDIUM ALT AND BODONI ANTIQUA T DEMI BOLD · PRINTED IN CHINA · ALL RIGHTS RESERVED. NO PART OF THIS BOOK MAY BE REPRODUCED, TRANSMITTED OR STORED IN AN INFORMATION RETRIEVAL SYSTEM IN ANY FORM OR BY ANY MEANS, GRAPHIC, ELECTRONIC OR MECHANICAL, INCLUDING PHOTOCOPYING, TAPING AND RECORDING, WITHOUT PRIOR WRITTEN PERMISSION FROM THE PUBLISHER. · BRITISH LIBRARY CATALOGUING IN PUBLICATION DATA: A CATALOGUE RECORD FOR THIS BOOK IS AVAILABLE FROM THE BRITISH LIBRARY · ISBN 978-1-4063-4532-2 · WWW.MALACHYDOYLE.COM · WWW.EDVERE.COM · WWW.WALKER.CO.UK

CRASH! JANGLE!

Meet the Bungles –
Whistle! Tweetle! Toot!
Mama Bungle *trills* and *tinkles,*
Papa **wheezes,** then he **sneezes,**
Granny Bungle *clicks* and *clacks*
and Grandpa Bill's a **boomer,**
Bella **bangs** on pots and pans
and Fitz and Finn,
the Bunglebabies,
Squeak and
Squawk and
SQUELCH!

Listen while I tell you
all about a bunch of Bungles –
they're a great enormous family
and they're noisy,
oh so noisy!

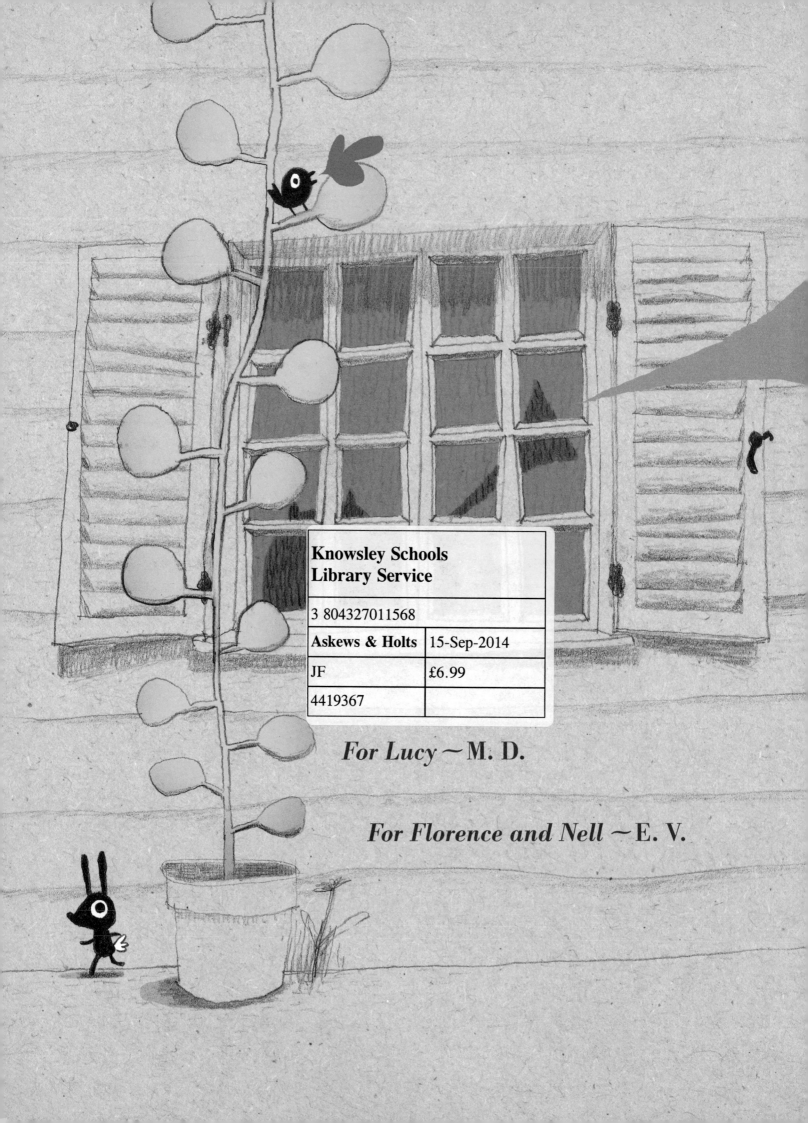

For Lucy ~ M. D.

For Florence and Nell ~ E. V.

"Oh, will you ever shush!" cried Sam,
the middle one, the quiet one,
the Bungle full of dreams.
"There isn't room to think round here,
all boom and bash and wallop!
Oh, I want it to be peaceful
but it's not – it never is!"

And so he upped

and so he offed

to the wood.

and so he wandered

"Aha!" he sighed,
"that's better," as he
looked around at clouds
and trees and greens
and blues and water.

He sat and looked,
and thought and looked,
and sat and hummed
a hum.

*"The sky is blue.
My shoe is, too!"*

"It rhymes!" said Sam.
"I like it!"

He had another little walk ...
then sat and looked,
and thought and looked,
and sat and hummed again.

"I can see a funny tree.
Stripy, just like Mama B!"

"It rhymes!" said Sam.
"I love it!"

Sam upped

and offed

and wandered

deeper, deep into the wood.

But **"Eeek!"** – he felt a creepy-crawly climbing up his trouser leg.

"Oooh," he said. "It's dark," he said. "I think I might be lost," he said.

Then **"*Beek!*"**
– he felt a flitter-flutter
flap around his face!
"Oooh," he said.
"I'm scared," he said.
"I wished I hadn't dared,"
he said, "go off alone,
all on my own."

Then

"Eeeky-beek!"

– a slippy-slidy
slithered
down his neck!

He opened up his lips

and then he opened up his mouth

and then he opened

up his throat

and *bellowed,*

Help!
Help!

He listened
and he listened
and ...

well, first
Sam heard a *little* sound –
a *trilling* and a *tinkling* ...

then he heard a bigger sound –
a **wheezing** and a **sneezing** ...

a **clicking** and a **clacking,**

then a **boomty-boomty-booming,**

growing **loud and loud again**

till it was like a ...

HURRICANE
of lovely **NOISE!**

The sun came through the trees
and so did Mama Bungle, Papa Bungle,
Grandpa Bill and Granny, too,
Bella banging pots and pans
and Fitz and Finn, the Bunglebabies –
Squeak, **Squawk**, **SQUELCH!**

"It's Sam," they yelled,
"we've found him!"

And they gathered all around him,
and they hugged him and they kissed him,
and they said how much they'd missed him.
He said he'd missed them too,
he said ...

"Although you're very loud,
you crowd, I'm glad to be a Bungle!"

Well, everybody cheered,
"HOORAY!"

And Sam was oh so happy,
for he loved them, every one.

"Quiet's good..." said Mama B.
"It is," said Sam, and nodded.
"But noisy's good as well sometimes –
especially when you're lost!"

And that's the ending,
happy ending.

That's the end.

This Faber book belongs to

FABER & FABER

has published children's books since 1929. Some of our very first publications included *Old Possum's Book of Practical Cats* by T. S. Eliot, starring the now world-famous Macavity, and *The Iron Man* by Ted Hughes. Our catalogue at the time said that 'it is by reading such books that children learn the difference between the shoddy and the genuine'. We still believe in the power of reading to transform children's lives.

For lovabubble Lizzie, adorabubble Jess and irreplaceabubble John
C. F.

For Annie & Casper
A. M.

First published in the UK in 2017, by Faber and Faber Limited, Bloomsbury House, 74–77 Great Russell Street, London WC1B 3DA. Text copyright © Clare Foges, 2017. Illustration copyright © Al Murphy, 2017. ISBN 978-0-571-33731-6 All rights reserved. Printed in Malta by Gutenberg Press Ltd.
1 3 5 7 9 10 8 6 4 2
The moral rights of Clare Foges and Al Murphy have been asserted. A CIP record for this book is available from the British Library.

When you kids go off to school,
And grown-ups go to work...

Your bathroom comes ALIVE
And all the things there go berserk!

The tiles become a dance floor,
The light a disco ball...

It's called the
BATHROOM BOOGIE
The most splashy bash of all!

SPLOT

SHAMPOO
gets things started,
She plays some funky beats.

TOOTHPASTE is the party king!
He loves to sing and shout.

He wriggles and he squeezes,

Until half his paste comes out!

He backflips on the bath mat...
And he shows them how to groove!

With twisty neck and silver suit...
Here comes the
POWER SHOWER!
He swings that neck from left to right—
It's shower's happy hour!

Every time he swings his head,
And FLICKS and FLOPS and FLIPS...
The shower gels run underneath
And rain dance in the drips!

The bubble bath is naughty!
She laughs when she's in trouble...

And every time she giggles—
POP! Out comes another bubble!

The **TOOTHBRUSHES** are ravers,
They blow on little whistles!
The sink becomes a mosh pit,
Where they headbang with their bristles...

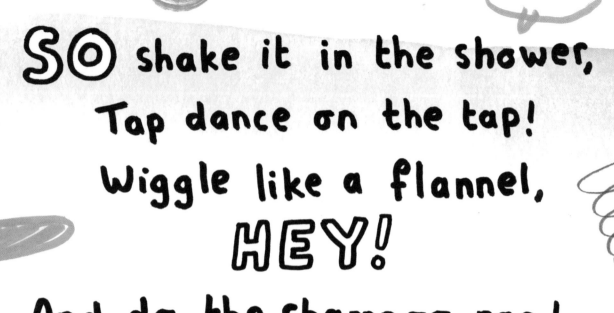

SO shake it in the shower,
Tap dance on the tap!
Wiggle like a flannel,
HEY!

And do the shampoo rap!

The BATH
becomes a pool party!
The SPONGES dive right in!

They team up with the
COTTON BUDS,
And synchronise a swim!

The **LOOFAHS** go bananas —
They dance like they don't care!
They limbo on the toilet lid...
And backflip through the air!

The SPONGES and the FLANNELS Are the very best of friends...

They do the hokey-cokey 'Til the bathroom boogie ends!

Shampoo tells them what to do:

Hey, quick! It's nearly three!
Let's clear this up and lickety-split
Before they're home for tea!

CLAP
CLAP

So if you're in the bathroom
And you notice something's moved...

You'll know it's from this party,
When your bathroom loves to groove!